Me, Stressed Out?

CollinsPublishersSanFrancisco

A Division of HarperCollins*Publishers*

Your Hair
Is The First
To Know

Life Can
Be A
Stress Test

Things Could Be Worse

What's Life
Without
Worries?

What's Life Without Worries?

A Packaged Goods Incorporated Book
First published 1996 by Collins Publishers San Francisco
1160 Battery Street, San Francisco, CA 94111-1213
http://www.harpercollins.com
Conceived and produced by Packaged Goods Incorporated
276 Fifth Avenue, New York, NY 10001
A Quarto Company

Library of Congress Cataloging-in-Publication Data
Schulz, Charles M.
[Peanuts. Selections]
Me, stressed out? / by Schulz.
p.   cm.
ISBN 0-00-225173-6
I. Title
PN6728.P4S3248   1996
741.5'973—dc20   96-16592
CIP

Printed in Hong Kong

1 3 5 7 9 10 8 6 4 2

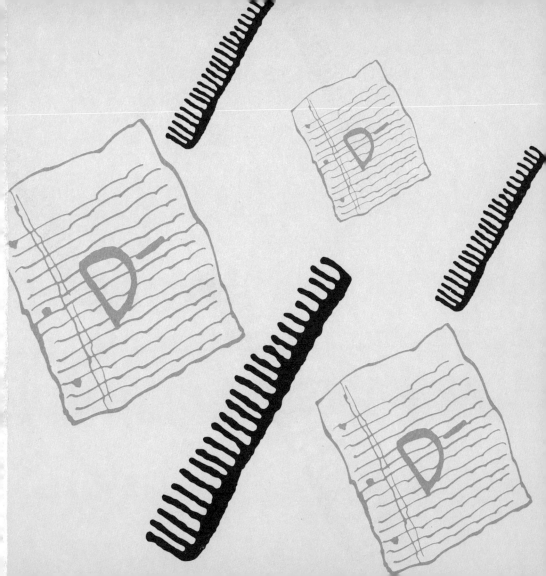

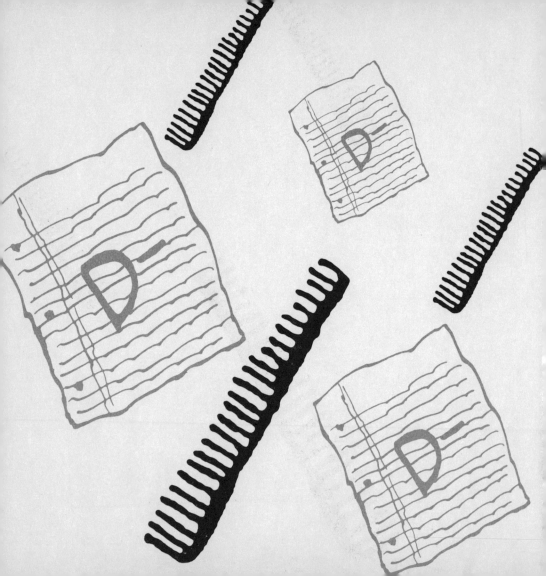